To Colby –

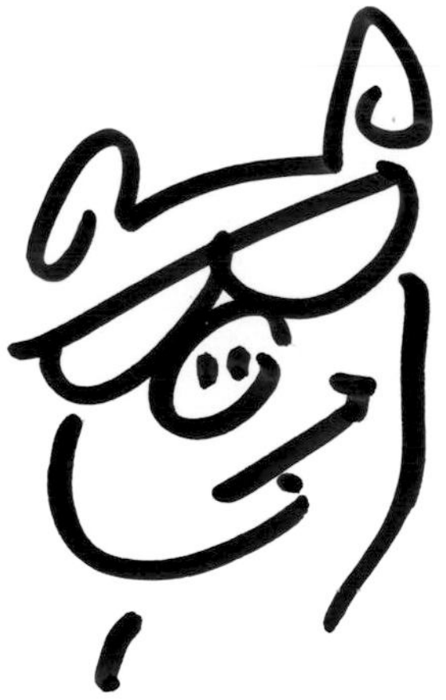

PUNK FARM
ON TOUR

JARRETT J. KROSOCZKA

Dragonfly Books ⸺🦟 New York

All rights reserved. Published in the United States by Dragonfly Books,
an imprint of Random House Children's Books, a division of Random House LLC,
a Penguin Random House Company, New York. Originally published in hardcover
in the United States by Alfred A. Knopf, an imprint of Random House Children's
Books, New York, in 2007.

Dragonfly Books with the colophon is a registered trademark of Random House LLC.

Visit us on the Web! randomhousekids.com

Educators and librarians, for a variety of teaching tools, visit us at RHTeachersLibrarians.com

The Library of Congress has cataloged the hardcover edition of this work as follows:
Krosoczka, Jarrett.
Punk farm on tour / Jarrett J. Krosoczka. — 1st ed.
p.   cm.
Summary: While Farmer Joe is at the National Tractor Society Conference in Reno, his animals go on tour
in a broken-down van, performing as the band called Punk Farm.
ISBN 978-0-375-83343-4 (trade) — ISBN 978-0-375-93343-1 (lib. bdg.) — ISBN 978-0-375-98525-6 (ebook)
[1. Rock music—Fiction. 2. Musicians—Fiction. 3. Domestic animals—Fiction.] I. Title.
PZ7.K935Pun 2007 [E]—dc22 2006035567

ISBN 978-0-553-50778-2 (pbk.)

MANUFACTURED IN CHINA

10 9 8 7 6 5 4 3 2 1

First Dragonfly Books Edition

For Diane and Joe

While Farmer Joe packs for the National Tractor Society Conference in Reno, Punk Farm gears up for their first big tour.

"We leave in a few days and we don't even have a killer song yet!" Chicken points out.

Cow taps a beat on her drums.
"Inspiration will hit."

"Guys, we have
something bigger
than songs to
worry about,"
interrupts Sheep.

"How are we going to get anywhere in a broken-down van?"

"And even more important, how are we going to get anywhere in *style* in that beat-up old thing?" adds Pig.

"I'll get this engine running, dude," says Goat.
"I guess we could paint the van," suggests Pig.
"I'll get the paint," offers Chicken.
"And I'll pack the instruments!" says Cow.
"This is going to be the best tour ever!"

Soon the Rock Van is ready to roll and Punk Farm
hits the road. Their first show is in Maine.
Finding Maine is easy. Finding their first show isn't.

"I think we should take a right," says Pig.
Sheep doesn't agree. "The map says to stay straight."
"We're *never* gonna get there on time!" cries Chicken.
"Chill, homie," *says* Goat.
"Everyone hold your horses!" Cow exclaims. "It's right up here!"

Backstage, Punk Farm is worried if the crowd
will like their new songs.
"I think I have our next big hit," says Sheep.
"Just follow my lead."
The club manager pokes his head in.
"You guys are on!"

"The wheels on the van go round and round!

Round and round!

Round and round!

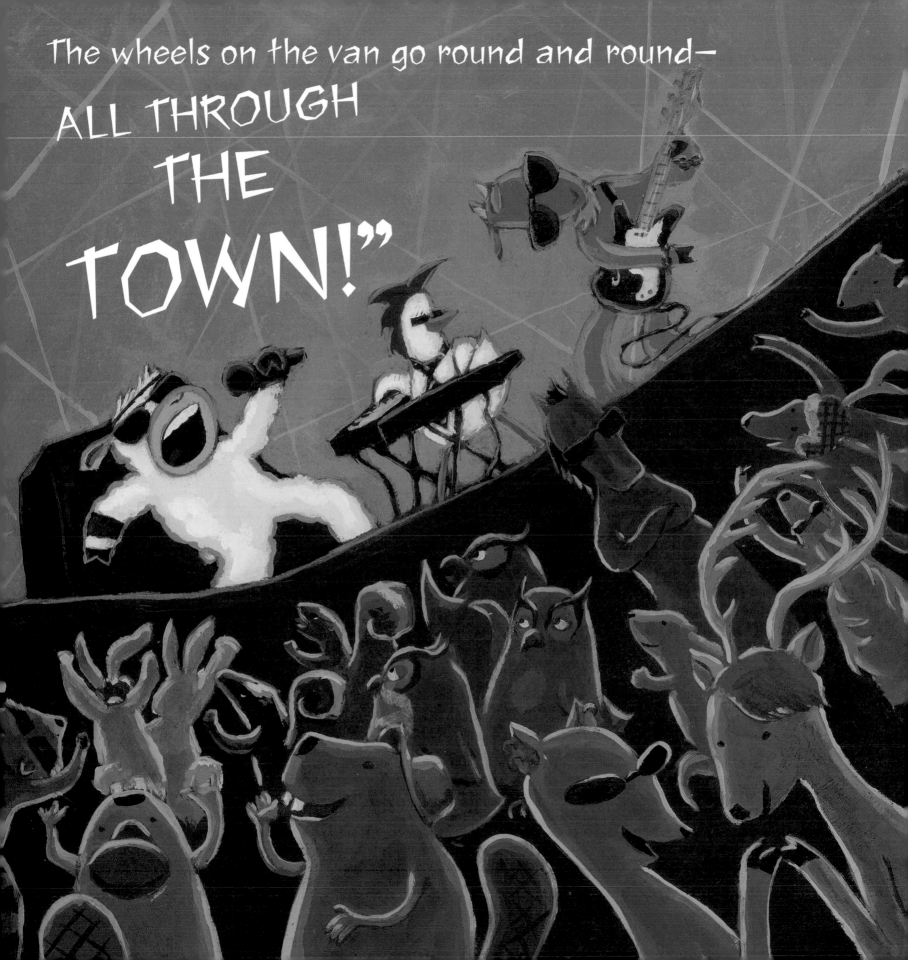

The wheels on the van go round and round—
ALL THROUGH
THE
TOWN!"

Their second show is in Florida. Their trip is slowed down by the rain.

"What if nobody comes because it's raining?" worries Chicken. Goat looks out the window. "The rain is beautiful, man."

"The wipers on the van go swish, swish, swish!
Swish, swish, swish!
Swish, swish, Swish!

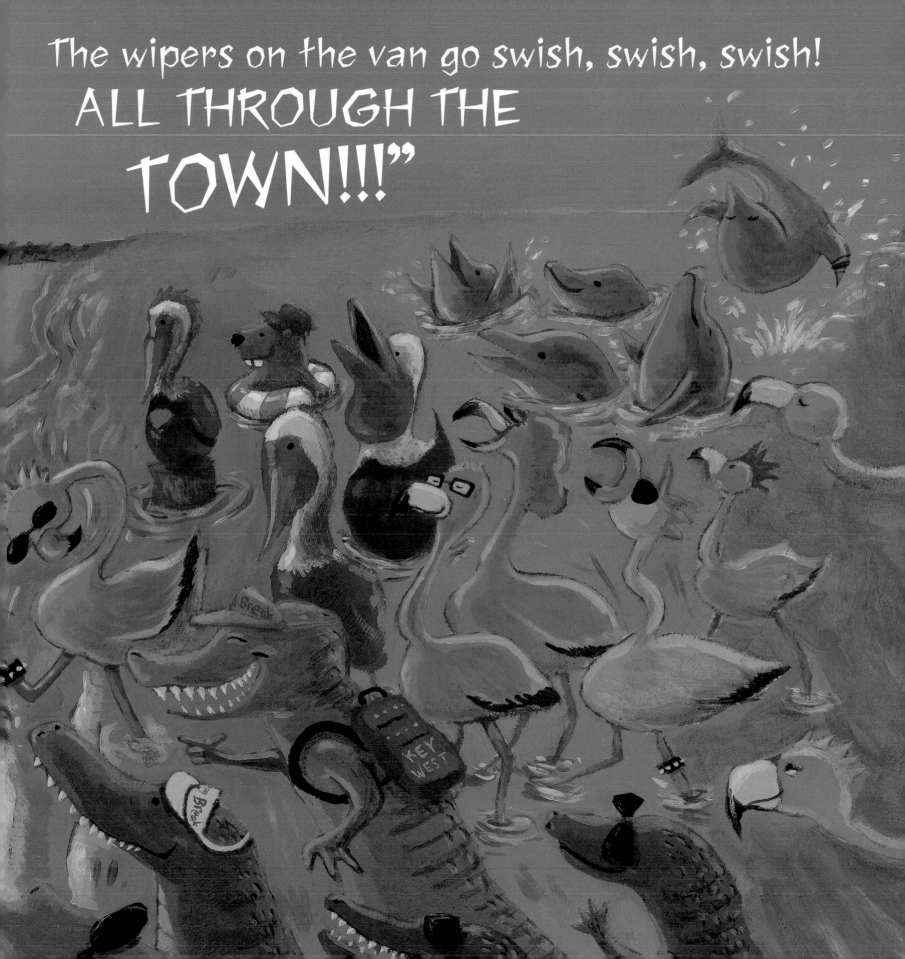

Cow high-fives everyone.
"We were awesome!" squeals
Chicken.
    "Pig? . . . Pig!!!" yells Sheep.

Things become tense when a tire pops on the way to Texas. "I'd help, but I don't want to get dirty," says Pig. "Just take the tire!" Cow pleads.

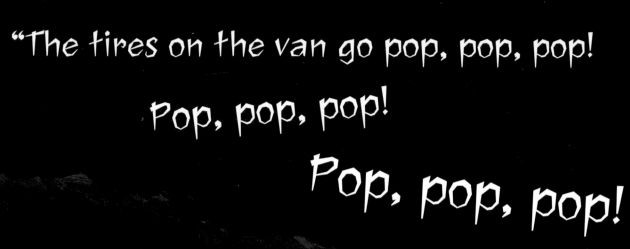

"The tires on the van go pop, pop, pop!

Pop, pop, pop!

Pop, pop, pop!

The tires on the van go **pop, pop, pop!**
ALL THROUGH THE *TOWN!!!*"

"We rocked it!" shouts Cow.
"PIG!" Sheep's patience is thin.

On the way to Colorado, the van breaks down.
Chicken throws her wings in the air. "We'll never make our last show!" Goat just shakes his head.
"This isn't good, is it?" asks Pig.

"The engine in the van goes clank, clank, clank!
Clank, clank, clank!

Clank, clank, clank!

The engine in the van goes clank, clank, clank!
ALL THROUGH THE . . .

Colorado!"

Punk Farm rushes offstage so they can get back home before Farmer Joe.

Farmer Joe heads home in an airplane.

Punk Farm races home in the Rock Van.

Who will get there first?

It's Punk Farm, without a second to spare!
"I sure did miss you guys while I was gone!" says
Farmer Joe. "Hope it wasn't too quiet on the farm!"